Letters from the Past

by Lillian Rose
illustrated by Larry Johnson

Orlando   Boston   Dallas   Chicago   San Diego

Visit *The Learning Site!*
www.harcourtschool.com

Except for one light in the back, the house was dark when Harriet got home from her violin lesson. She shook the snow off her cap and hung it up with her coat, then removed her boots. She placed them outside in the little closed-in porch that most Vermonters call the "mud room." Then she called out to her father.

"Dad, I'm home!"

"Hi, sugar!" her father called. "Come on back here. There's something I want to show you."

Harriet made her way to her father's study, where he was sitting at his desk, papers scattered all over. He was examining what must have been the contents of the large manila envelope now lying on the floor. Harriet stooped to pick it up, glancing idly at the return address, which was somewhere in South Carolina. She handed the envelope to her father and sat down opposite him.

Mr. Robinson looked up at his daughter over his reading glasses, an unspoken question on his face.

"Mom dropped me off and headed back to the hospital," Harriet said. "The woman she operated on this morning is out of recovery and back in her room, and Mom wanted to check up on her. She says—"

"I know," her father finished for her, smiling. "She won't be long if there are no complications. Well, we can always reheat the lasagna if she's late."

"Are you doing some research on the South?" The courses her father taught at the community college were about American history, so she assumed he'd sent for some information from South Carolina.

"Not exactly, though this certainly is a significant part of American history. All this material actually concerns you, so come around here and let me show you what I've received."

3

She went and stood next to her father, peering over his shoulder at the papers he'd been reading.

"I've been doing some research on the Robinson family in South Carolina, hoping I could unearth some information on pre-Civil War times."

"I thought our family had been living in Vermont even before it became a state."

Her father nodded and said, "Yes, at least that's true of my mother's family—your grandmother Harriet, whose namesake you are. They were farmers who settled here in 1777, when Vermont adopted its first constitution, which abolished all slavery."

Harriet smiled at her father's lecture-hall tone.

"Sorry, sugar, I guess you've heard all that before. What you haven't heard, though, is the information in these letters, about my *father's* family."

Harriet looked more closely at the papers her father had been examining. Only then did she realize that they were photocopies of letters, very old letters, hand-written in a beautiful script that was surprisingly easy to read, except for those places where the original letters must have been folded. Some of the writing was blurred, too, and hard to decipher, as though the ink had faded over time.

"These are copies of letters received by a woman named Alice Southworth in South Carolina from a certain Judith Freeman in Vermont beginning in the year 1868. Does that ring any bells?" he asked, smiling as though he already knew the answer.

"Yes," said Harriet excitedly, "that's great-great—" She had forgotten how many *greats* there were before the word *grandmother*. What she did know was that Judith Freeman was one of her ancestors. She also remembered the excitement last year when the family unearthed the one surviving letter from Alice Southworth in a trunk that had been passed down through the generations.

"That's right, and a few months ago I took a chance and began corresponding with some Southworth descendants whose addresses I found on the Internet. This package of goodies came today: copies of some of the letters Judith Freeman wrote to Alice not too long after she—that is, Judith—reached Vermont."

"What do they say? What do they tell about Grandmother Freeman? Did you learn anything new?" Harriet's questions tumbled out.

"Well, I'm just going to let you read them and find out for yourself. I know some of the writing's hard to decipher, but I think you won't have any trouble following the story."

Harriet took several pages from her father, handling them as though they were something precious, which in a way they were. She burrowed into an easy chair, turned on a reading lamp, and, under that flood of light, stepped back into an earlier time.

Dearest Alice,

My dear, dear friend, I only hope that this letter finds you well, though what I most desire is that it finds you at all. Yes, it is I, your old friend Judith, greeting you again, though I never had the opportunity to say good-bye. When I left South Carolina with the others, there was no time for farewells, only the pressing need for secrecy and silence. That was how it was for us all the way North. We, of course, made our brave exodus by means of what is still known as the Underground Railroad.

I left South Carolina a child, being only fourteen years old, and I left without my family. My mother's health, never robust, kept her at the Longwood plantation, where she felt she must tend to the youngest Longwood child and the other children orphaned when Mrs. Sarah O'Marah, who you will remember as Miss Longwood, died shortly after childbirth. The only kin the children had left were elderly aunts and the men still at war fighting for the South. My mother felt she had a duty to them.

My older brother, Benjamin, was determined to stay with Mother, at least until he could find some way to join the Union forces, and thus help end the bitter war and secure the freedom of all our people.

Yes, when I left South Carolina, you knew me to be as uneducated as an infant. What I never revealed, though, not even to you, was that this was a false picture. The young Mrs. O'Marah, when she was still Miss Longwood, was more daring than you might have believed her to be. Though she knew it was unlawful, she taught me the magic of reading, swearing me to secrecy. You see, one day she found me in the library, where I was supposed to be dusting, only instead I was opening one book after another and straining to interpret the printed symbols.

I think she liked the sense of danger and mystery in participating in something so forbidden, or perhaps she just enjoyed the very act of teaching— that is, writing on a blank slate, so to speak, and leaving her mark there.

Harriet looked up from her reading to ask her father what Judith's reference to "forbidden" meant.

He removed his glasses and polished them as he explained. "There were laws that said that no one could teach a slave how to read or write. The men who framed those laws understood that whoever had knowledge would both crave freedom and be able to support himself—or herself—in a free world."

Her father was sounding like a professor again, but somehow the tone seemed appropriate for the moment.

"The slate, then—that's what students wrote on, wasn't it?" she asked, though she understood that Grandmother Freeman was using the expression as a figure of speech. Her father nodded, and Harriet returned to her reading.

Once Miss Longwood became Mrs. O'Marah, that all ended, as you can well understand. Her time was occupied first by her new husband, and soon enough with her young children. I could do little to advance my knowledge until I came to Vermont and was able to study further.

Harriet looked up at her father, who patiently interrupted his own reading to respond to her questions. "Her writing's so different, Daddy, so elegant." She was comparing it to the brief e-mail messages she dashed off every day, which never sounded like this!

"Yes, it's definitely more formal than what most of us are used to today—unless, of course," he added with a laugh, "you're a person like me who's always studying old books and letters."

Harriet went back to her reading. She'd been able to decipher most of the words and use the context to figure out the ones that were indistinct. The letter went on, but the tone of it had changed.

So my dear Alice, I have given you mostly details of my own life, and while I sincerely yearn to learn more of your own fate, I write in hopes that you can enlighten me about the two other people I hold dear. Yes, I am speaking of my mother, Naomi, and my brother, Benjamin. If you know anything of them, I beseech you to share that knowledge with me, be it good or ill. I trust that my faith will make me strong enough to bear any bad news, because my hope of hearing good tidings gives me the strength to bear whatever reports I do hear.

The letter ended with the simple closing "With love, J."

"Oh, Daddy," Harriet exclaimed, shuffling the papers in her hand, "I just have to know what happened next."

"Okay, Miss Historian, don't panic," her father said, smiling as he counted out a few more pages from the pile and handed them to Harriet. "This will bring you up to date, or at least almost as far as I've read myself."

Harriet took the pages eagerly and discovered they were copies of a letter dated several months after the first one. She skimmed the pages quickly because she felt that she couldn't bear to read the letter unless she knew in advance what the news would be. She read just enough to believe it might be hopeful. Thus, although the letter began with the same greeting, it somehow had a joyous ring to it.

Dearest Alice,

How good it was to receive your letter and know it was from your very own hand. I almost couldn't bear to open it at first and just held it close to me in the knowledge that it had come from you. You are married to George Southworth! I knew when I saw the return address that it was you, even though I had just hopefully addressed my letter to Alice Trumbull and prayed that someone there would know how to direct it.

That you received the letter would almost have been wonder enough, but that you could actually send me the tidings I sought—it is too wonderful. Though it's been two years since you saw my mother, you say she was well and looking forward to traveling North with Benjamin when he returned from service in the Union Army. I knew, of course, that our late President Lincoln began to welcome freed black men into the army as early as 1863 and, given my brother's desire to serve, nothing would have stopped him from enlisting, short of my mother's ill health. Therefore, she must have been well enough for him to be willing to leave.

"Great-Uncle Benjamin was in the Union Army!" declared Harriet, though she knew her father had already read the letter.

"Yes, along with about 200,000 other African American men. Now I'll say 'Read on' before you start asking me even more questions that the letter itself will answer!"

The main question, of course, was whether Great-Uncle Benjamin had survived the war, and the answer was in the very next paragraph.

I am so touched by the story of your efforts to locate my mother and brother, though I know you tell me of it in detail to assure me that your efforts were thorough, not to win my praise. However, I can only draw the same conclusions as you did after your visit to the Longwood plantation. You say you found all the children grown except the youngest, and only their father and new stepmother remained. They knew nothing of my mother, only that she had been "gone these two years." I can understand how your heart might have nearly stopped at the word "gone," until you learned that it meant only that she had departed the area. My own pulse missed a beat or two until I read ahead.

I must believe that Benjamin returned and that together he and Mother went their own way as only a free people might. I feel in my heart that they have migrated North, but how far—that is yet to be discovered.

Dearest friend, I will read your letter over and over for any clue it might offer. Keep me in your thoughts until you can write again, with or without news.

With love, J

Harriet looked up at her father and said, "Daddy, it's like reading an adventure story in installments! I will absolutely burst if you don't tell me what happened."

"Well, don't do that!" her father teased. "I would prefer that you learn from the letters, just as I've been doing, but I *will* give you a hint."

With that, he handed Harriet a computer printout. All the pages were connected to form one continuous sheet that unfolded like an accordion.

"You know the family tree I've been working on since—"

"Since forever, practically," Harriet finished for him with a laugh. The family tree had been the main topic of conversation at every family gathering for years, and still it wasn't complete.

"Well, I guess it's probably more interesting to me, the family's designated historian, than to my poor, suffering daughter," her father said with a grin. He looked through the pages until he found the one he wanted.

"Here," he said, pointing to an item about one-third of the way down the accordion.

Harriet looked at where her father pointed. "It's Great-Uncle Benjamin, and it says he lived in—Boston! So he wasn't far away at all! That's cool, but—" she paused, then finished—"but that doesn't tell us if he and his sister, I mean Grandmother Freeman, were ever reunited."

Her father didn't answer. He just handed her more papers.

"Dearest friend," the next letter began, "dear carrier of good news, I have found them, I have found them, thanks to your determined efforts."

"Oh, Daddy," she said, her eyes filling with tears, "it's like, it's like—I don't know, I guess it's like being right there with Judith when she wrote this."

"Well, maybe we'll make a historian of you yet, Harriet. I think you've gotten a sense of the excitement I experience when I learn about people's lives, though of course this is even more special, being our own ancestor."

"I know I'm going to read every one of these letters two or three times, maybe more, but as for being another historian, I'm not sure." She waved her arms as though playing a violin and said, "I'll have to see if I can fit it in around my concert schedule."